Original concept by
Roger Hargreaves

Written and illustrated by
Adam Hargreaves

Little Miss Curious had found a footprint.

The biggest footprint she had ever seen and she could not imagine what had made it. So she asked Mr Clever.

"That's a dinosaur footprint," explained Mr Clever.

There's not much that Mr Clever doesn't know.

"I wonder what dinosaurs look like," wondered Little Miss Curious.

"Let's go and have a look," suggested Mr Clever.

So they followed the footprints.

"Where are you two going?" asked Mr Greedy.

"We're off to find dinosaurs," replied Mr Clever.

"That sounds like fun," said Mr Greedy and he joined them. Along with a lot of their other friends who they met on the way.

It's not every day you get the chance to see a dinosaur!

The dinosaurs were more extraordinary than even
Mr Clever had imagined they would be.

They were taller than Mr Tall.

"This must be how Mr Small feels all the time," said
Mr Tall, looking up at the Brachiosaurus.

"Imagine how small I feel now!" squeaked Mr Small.

The dinosaurs were stronger than Mr Strong.

Try as he might, Mr Strong could not move
the Ankylosaurus.

It was built like a brick wall!

And the dinosaurs were even greedier than Mr Greedy.

He watched in astonishment as an Apatosaurus ate
a whole tree.

"That would be like me eating a whole field of lettuce!"
said Mr Greedy.

But the dinosaurs were not naughtier than
Little Miss Naughty!

"These dinosaurs just eat plants," complained
Mr Greedy. "I want to see a proper meat-eating dinosaur."

These were words that Mr Greedy quickly regretted as
at that very moment a Tyrannosaurus Rex came stomping
out of the forest and decided that Mr Greedy looked like
a good-sized snack!

"Oh help!" shrieked Mr Greedy, running as fast as his little legs would carry him.

But a Tyrannosaurus Rex has much longer legs.

And sharp teeth.

And even sharper claws.

Run, Mr Greedy! Run for your life!

Luckily for Mr Greedy it turned out that the Tyrannosaurus
Rex was ticklish.

Mr Tickle had never tickled anything so large before. It had taken every inch of those extraordinarily long arms of his.

Mr Tickle wondered what other dinosaurs he could tickle.

He tickled a Triceratops behind the collar.

He needed long arms to keep out of the way of those horns.

He tickled a Diplodocus under the chin.

And he tickled a Stegosaurus.

"I didn't know that dinosaurs could giggle," giggled Little Miss Giggles.

She also did not know that dinosaurs laid eggs.

"I would only need one of those eggs for breakfast," said
Mr Strong.

By the time Little Miss Curious got home, she was not nearly as curious as she had been at the start of the day.

What a lot she had learnt about dinosaurs.

"Just one more question," she said. "What do dinosaurs dream about?"

Mr Clever sighed a heavy sigh.

There are just some things that even Mr Clever does not know!